Pete's Peculiar Pet Shop

I Want a Unicorn!

Written by Sheila May Bird

Illustrated by Jim Field

"I want a unicorn!" shouted the princess. She shouted so loudly that the maid had to put her fingers in her ears.

"And I **always** get what I want!" the princess added. She stamped her feet. She stamped them so hard that the butler fell over.

"Wherever can we get a unicorn?" asked the queen.

"From Pete's Peculiar Pet Shop," said the king.

4

The king did not visit Pete's Peculiar Pet Shop in his golden coach. He did not want a fuss, so he went on the bus.

"Your Majesty," said Pete, bowing low.

"Your Majesty," said the Griffin, bowing his head.

"Your Majesty," said Mopsy, trying to curtsy.

"The princess wants a unicorn," said the king, "and the princess always gets what she wants."

Pete did not have a unicorn,
so he put a sign in the window.

Unicorn
wanted for
princess
who always
gets what
she wants

A tall man came into the shop.
"I have a unicorn for sale," he said.
"That is not a unicorn," sneered the
Griffin. "That is a donkey. A unicorn
has a horn on its forehead."

A tall lady entered the shop.

"I have a unicorn for sale," she said.

"That is not a unicorn," said the Griffin. "That is the same donkey with an ice-cream cone on its forehead."

A little girl pushed open the shop door.
"I'm Sally and I have a unicorn," she said.
"I expect it's just a donkey with an ice-cream cone on its head," the Griffin snorted.
"No," said Sally. "I know it's a unicorn because my grandpa said so."

10

"Do you want to sell your unicorn?" asked Pete.

"No," said Sally. "I love my unicorn, but I cannot keep it. It is too big now to live in our garden. The princess has a big garden and I know my unicorn would love to live in a big garden."

Please
keep pets
on a lead.
Thank you.

13

Pete told the king about Sally's unicorn.

The king told the queen about Sally's unicorn.

The queen told the princess about Sally's unicorn.

The princess told **everybody** about *her* unicorn.

Pete and Sally took the unicorn to the palace.

"That's *my* unicorn!" shouted the princess. "I want it, and I **always** get what I want."

The princess yelled so loudly that the unicorn ran away.

15

"Bring back *my* unicorn!" shouted the princess, but the more the princess screamed, the further the unicorn ran.

The princess stamped her feet. The princess lay on the ground and kicked.

The princess bellowed,

"I WANT MY UNICORN!"

"But I don't think the unicorn wants you," said Pete.

Everyone looked at
the princess.

"I want my unicorn,"
repeated the princess,
but she stopped kicking.

"I want my ..." She
stood up.

"I want ..." She looked
at everyone looking at her.

"And ... I'm not going
to get what I want,
am I?"

"No!" shouted everyone.

They walked back to the castle, leaving Sally alone with the princess.

"*I'll* show you how to call him," said Sally. She whistled loudly.

"Can I try that?" asked the princess.

Sally showed her how to whistle. The princess had never whistled before. It was fun.

Sally showed the princess
how to feed the unicorn ...

and how to ride the unicorn.

The princess asked Sally, "Would you come and help me look after the unicorn? We could share it."

"Yes, please," said Sally. "We can be friends."

The princess had never had a friend before. It was fun.

"I want you to be my friend," said the princess. She grinned and added, "And I always get what I want!"